Secret
Kingdom

Special thanks to Anna Bowles

For Emma Collier,
who loves to play in the snow!

ORCHARD BOOKS
338 Euston Road, London NW1 3BH
Orchard Books Australia
Level 17/207 Kent Street, Sydney, NSW 2000
A Paperback Original

First published in 2012 by Orchard Books

A CIP catalogue record for this book is available
from the British Library.

ISBN 978 1 40832 368 7

9 10

Printed and bound by CPI Group (UK) Ltd, Croydon, CR0 4YY

The paper and board used in this paperback are natural recyclable
products made from wood grown in sustainable forests. The
manufacturing processes conform to the environmental regulations
of the country of origin.

Orchard Books is a division of Hachette Children's Books,
an Hachette UK company

www.hachette.co.uk

Series created by Hothouse Fiction
www.hothousefiction.com

Magic Mountain

ROSIE BANKS

ORCHARD

Contents

A Night-Time Adventure   9

Magic Mountain   29

Everwarm Embers   45

Summer's Idea   63

A Race Against Time   75

Snowboarding Sprites   89

Snowy Fun!   103

A Night-Time Adventure

"I'm Queen Malice!" cried the girl in black. She shook her long, dark hair back from her face. "Get them, Storm Sprites!" Two small creatures with black wings ran into the room and cackled nastily.

Summer Hammond and Ellie Macdonald squealed and dived over the playroom sofa. The girl in black was only their friend Jasmine, dressed in an old sheet and waving a thunderbolt made from a painted stick. But her acting was so good that it almost seemed like nasty Queen Malice was in the room!

The Storm Sprites were Summer's little brothers, Finn and Connor, dressed up to look like Queen Malice's horrible grey-skinned, spiky-fingered helpers. Ellie had tucked old towels into their T-shirts and folded them in the shape of the Storm Sprites' bat-like wings.

The boys shrieked with excitement and ran across the room to grab Summer's legs as she tried to scrunch herself up behind the sofa.

"Got you!" Connor giggled.

"That's what you think," laughed Summer, jumping up and tickling him. Ellie did the same to Finn.

"Foolish sprites!" scolded Jasmine in a dramatic voice. "Do I have to do everything myself?" She poked Summer playfully with the thunderbolt stick.

"Connor, Finn!" Summer's step-dad called from the kitchen. "Bath time!"

Summer let Connor go and went to the door. "They're coming!" she called back. "Sorry, guys," she told her little brothers. "We have to stop playing now."

"But I want to be a Storm Sprite,"

said three-year-old Finn, sticking out his bottom lip.

"Storm Sprites aren't real, silly," five-year-old Connor told him scornfully.

Summer grinned at Jasmine and Ellie over her brothers' heads. Little did the boys know that Storm Sprites *were* real, and that they lived in a magical land called the Secret Kingdom!

The Secret Kingdom was a wonderful place full of pixies, unicorns, mermaids and all kinds of magical creatures, but it was in trouble – and only Ellie, Summer and Jasmine could help.

One day not very long ago, the girls had found a magical box at a school jumble sale that had transported King Merry, the ruler of the Secret Kingdom, and his royal pixie, Trixi, to the human world. King Merry and Trixi had asked the girls for their help in stopping Queen Malice, the king's evil sister, from causing trouble in the kingdom.

Queen Malice had been so angry when King Merry had been chosen to rule the Secret Kingdom instead of her that she had hidden six horrible thunderbolts around the land. She had cast spells on each of the thunderbolts so they would cause chaos and ruin all the fun in the kingdom.

Jasmine, Ellie and Summer had already found four of the thunderbolts and broken their nasty spells. But until the Magic Box called them into the kingdom again, all they could do was *play* at fighting Queen Malice and the Storm Sprites!

Summer, Ellie and Jasmine helped Finn and Connor take off their costumes, then sent them off to have a bath.

The girls headed up towards Summer's room to watch a DVD. As they passed the big window in the hall, they saw it was dark and snowy outside.

"Maybe it will snow again tonight," said Jasmine hopefully.

"Brrrr," said Ellie, pushing her wiry red curls back from her face as she looked into the gloomy garden. "Perfect weather for a sleepover!" she grinned.

They went into Summer's room, which was painted a soft yellow and had lots of animal posters all over the walls. Summer put on her comfy old yellow flowered pyjamas. Ellie got into her green and purple pair and then they both admired

Jasmine's shorts and vest set, which were brand new and covered with big pink polka dots.

"What shall we watch?" said Summer, looking through her pile of DVDs.

But Jasmine and Ellie weren't paying attention. They had taken the Magic Box down from among the rows of books and piles of stuffed toys on Summer's tall bookcase and put it on top of Ellie's sleeping bag.

The Magic Box was about the size of a jewellery box. Its wooden sides were carved with pictures of magical creatures, and it had a mirror set into its curved lid, which was surrounded by six beautiful green gemstones.

"I know what I'd like to watch," said Ellie. "The Magic Box shining!"

"Ooh, yes!" agreed Jasmine, tracing the carvings with her finger. "And a riddle appearing to tell us where the next thunderbolt is!"

Jasmine lay on her front and stared

at the box, willing a message to appear, until her eyes watered. "It's no good!" she said finally. "Let's just put a film on."

Summer put a DVD in, and the girls ended up laughing so much that Mrs Hammond had to come in and tell them it was bedtime. After that they talked in whispers for a while, then one by one they drifted off to sleep.

In the middle of the night, Summer suddenly woke up. Blinking sleepily, she looked around to find out what had disturbed her.

Ellie and Jasmine were curled up in their sleeping bags on the floor, and everything looked normal. Then Summer realised what was strange – the fact that she could see at all! Instead of being dark, her room was lit up by a dim glow.

But it can't be morning already, she thought. Then she glanced up at her shelves and her heart jumped with excitement – the light was coming from the Magic Box!

Suddenly feeling wide awake, she slipped out of bed and crept between the two sleeping bags that were taking up most of her floor. With trembling hands, she nudged Ellie and Jasmine.

"The Magic Box," she whispered, reaching up to get it. "It's glowing!"

Ellie and Jasmine woke up and quickly

scrambled out of their sleeping bags.

As the girls gathered around the box, light flickered across their faces and words began to form in the mirror on its lid:

Where the brownies slide, not run,
Where they ride on boards for fun,
Where cheeks are red
and breath is white,
That's where you must go tonight!

"Surfing brownies?" whispered Summer uncertainly. "That would explain the boards. But not the red cheeks and white breath."

"I know!" Ellie gasped. "Surfing isn't the only sport that uses a board. My uncle went *snow*boarding last month."

"And when it's cold and snowy, you can see your breath and your cheeks go red!" Jasmine cried loudly.

"Shhh!" Summer told her, giggling. "You'll wake up my mum!"

"Sorry," Jasmine whispered as quietly

as she could. "We must be going where there are snowboarding brownies!"

"Look, the Magic Box is opening," said Ellie.

The girls watched as the curved lid of the box opened to reveal six little compartments inside. Four of them were already filled with the amazing gifts that they'd been given for helping the Secret Kingdom. There was a magical moving map that showed what was happening in the whole of the kingdom, a tiny silver unicorn horn that let them talk to animals, a beautiful crystal that could control the weather and a pearl that made anyone who held it temporarily invisible.

Ellie reached carefully inside and took out the map King Merry had given them

on their first visit. She spread it out on
her sleeping bag so that it was lit by the
glow from the Magic Box.

Summer and Jasmine leant forward
eagerly.

"What about here?" Ellie pointed.
At the very bottom of the
crescent moon-shaped
island was a huge
mountain, capped
with sparkly
pink snow!
As the girls
watched, the
map showed
the pink
snowflakes
falling thickly
around it. At the

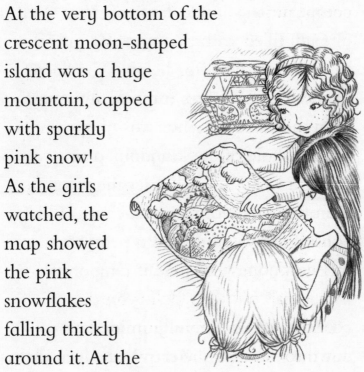

bottom of the mountain they could just make out a little town.

"There's a place name, but what does it say?" Summer murmured. "It's so dark I can't see."

Jasmine leant right over the map and peered at it.

"Got it!" she shouted out. "It's called Magic Mountain."

"Shhh!" whispered Summer, frowning at Jasmine.

Jasmine sat back and slapped one hand over her mouth. The girls listened, but there was no sound from the rest of the house.

"Phew," whispered Ellie.

The girls put their palms on the beautiful green stones. Jasmine leant down to whisper the answer to the riddle.

"Magic Mountain," she said, so quietly the others could barely hear her.

Everything was silent for a moment, but then the girls heard a strange rustling noise. It seemed to be coming from behind Summer's curtains…

Suddenly the material twitched aside, and a tiny pixie flew into Summer's bedroom, riding on a leaf! Her messy blonde hair was tucked under a flower hat, and her dress was made out of little green leaves, neatly stitched together. She wore a pretty fur-lined cape, and a ring twinkled on her finger like a star in the night.

"It's Trixibelle!" Summer whispered delightedly.

"Oh, my," the pixie whispered. "I must be back in the Other Realm. But it's so dark! Are you there, girls?"

Trixi tapped her ring and the string of lights that hung at the top of Summer's curtains suddenly lit up the room with a pretty pink glow.

"I thought they were called *fairy* lights!" Ellie giggled.

"Those ones are pixie lights!" Trixi grinned as she swooped over to kiss the girls on their noses.

"We've worked out where the next

thunderbolt is, Trixi," Summer told their
tiny pixie friend excitedly. "It's at Magic
Mountain!"

"Horrid Queen Malice," murmured
the little pixie crossly. "We must go at
once." She went to touch her ring, then
hesitated, looking at the girls. "Oh, but
you can't go dressed like that! Stand still
for a moment."

There was a brief flash and a twinkling
sound. The girls looked down to find
themselves wearing coats, boots, scarves,
gloves and earmuffs, all the same colours
as their pyjamas! On their heads were the
sparkly tiaras that magically appeared
every time they visited the Secret
Kingdom, which showed everyone who
saw them that they were Very Important
Friends of King Merry's.

"Perfect," Trixi said approvingly. "Now we're ready for snow!"

Magic Mountain

Trixi tapped her ring to summon the
magical whirlwind that would transport
them all to the Secret Kingdom, and
chanted:

"The evil queen has trouble planned.
Brave helpers fly to save our land!"

Ellie held on to Jasmine and tried not to worry as she felt herself tumbling through the air. If tonight was anything like their other visits to the kingdom, they would be sure to arrive high up in the air, and she was afraid of heights!

But as the wind died down, Ellie felt something solid beneath her feet. "Thank goodness!" she exclaimed as she opened her eyes. Straight away she wished she hadn't!

The whirlwind had put them down right at the top of the snow-covered mountain they'd seen on the map. Ellie could see a town far off in the distance at the base of the mountain, but it looked tiny from so high up.

It was already dawn in the Secret Kingdom, and the sun was starting to rise gently above the mountaintops, making the pink snowflakes twinkle in the air.

"It's so beautiful!" Jasmine gasped.

"Are we going all the way down there?" Summer asked, pointing towards the town.

"Yes," said Trixi with a smile. "But don't worry – it won't take long at all!" She tapped her ring and suddenly each of the girls had a pair of skis strapped to her feet. Summer's were yellow, Jasmine's were pink and Ellie's were purple.

"Wheeee!" cried Jasmine, pushing off with her ski poles and sliding down the hill.

"Jasmine, come back!" shouted Ellie in alarm. "I can't ski!"

"I don't think Jasmine can either," said Summer. "But she's doing it anyway!"

Jasmine turned around and waved happily at her friends, but she couldn't ski back uphill to join them.

"Don't worry," said Trixi. "I'll put a spell on your skis to make sure they carry you safely down the slope." She pointed her ring towards the girls' feet, and a burst of glittery dust shot out and settled over their skis. "There now," she said. "Try them out."

"All right," Ellie said to Summer. "Give me a push!"

Summer gave Ellie a gentle shove and then set off down the hill behind her. It was a bit scary, but the magic skis worked wonderfully. Ellie and Summer's feet stayed safely on the snow, and soon they drew level with Jasmine.

As the girls skied along next to one another, they looked around in wonder.

"I want to have a go on those!" said Jasmine, pointing to a set of long ice slides that looped and curled all the way down the mountain.

Summer didn't answer. She was busy watching a herd of reindeer that were galloping through the sky towards a distant wood. Their hooves gave off sparks of magic as they flew through the air!

"I never thought I'd actually get to see flying reindeer!" Ellie grinned.

The girls skied all the way down the mountain into the town below. It was a perfect winter scene, with beautiful snow-covered houses and cafés all laid out in a square. There were even pretty little igloos, which were a glittering pink colour just like the snow they were made from.

"Even the cafés look like snowballs!"
Ellie grinned.

But as Summer looked around the
pretty town, she got a funny feeling.
"Where is everyone?" she asked warily.

The snowball cafés were shut and
several snowboards, sleds and skis had
been left lying outside as if they'd been
abandoned in a hurry. Wind whistled
eerily all around the mountainside.

"That's strange," said Trixi, who was
flying along beside the girls on her
snowflake. "Magic Mountain is usually a
lot busier than this."

"It must have something to do with
Queen Malice's thunderbolt," Jasmine
said. "We'd better see if we can find it."

They carried on, skiing down a slope
that was lined with realistic-looking
ice sculptures. There were reindeer and
penguins and seals, and even a big
polar bear.

"Hey!" said Jasmine. She pointed at one
of the ice statues and frowned. "I'm sure

that penguin just waved its wing at me!"

"I expect it did," Trixi smiled. "Those statues are magical. The snow brownies make them. It's because of the brownies that Magic Mountain is such a fun place to visit."

The girls hurried over to take a closer look at the statues.

"Hello!" said Ellie, shaking the polar bear's frozen paw.

The bear moved his head from side to side. He seemed to be looking for something.

"Are you wondering where all the brownies have gone?" asked Jasmine.

The statue nodded slowly in reply.

"Don't worry," Summer told him. "We'll find out what's going on."

As the girls skied onwards, Trixi flew back and forth across the street, peering in through the shuttered windows of the snug-looking igloos that lined it.

"Brrr," Summer said, her teeth chattering. Even with her cosy ski jacket and earmuffs on, she was still very cold. "Maybe the snow brownies are off somewhere keeping warm."

"But shouldn't *snow* brownies like the cold?" Jasmine asked.

"They do," Trixi told them. "But when it gets too cold the snow turns to ice, and so do the snow brownies," she continued sadly. "They wear ember necklaces to keep them warm enough while they're playing outside. They even use everwarm ember coals to heat the igloos and cafes. The embers are magical – they keep everyone warm, but don't make the snow melt."

"That sounds nice," said Jasmine, shivering. "I think we need to find some everwarm ember necklaces of our own to warm ourselves up!"

Trixi looked around at all the empty igloos. "Normally there'd be lots of brownies here, but I don't know where they've all gone."

She sighed, and then brightened up. "I

know! Let's go and see King Merry at his winter palace. He might know what's happened. Every winter he comes skiing at Magic Mountain, even though he's not very good at it." She winked at the girls.

"Last year he fell over so much he caused an avalanche!" she added with a giggle.

Ellie, Summer and Jasmine smiled, even though their teeth were chattering. They were always glad to see the friendly king – and they would be very pleased indeed to get out of the freezing cold!

On their way to the palace, they skied past a big lake full of very clear ice.

"Something's definitely wrong," said Trixi. "That's Ice-Skate Lake. There are always brownies playing on it. I've never seen it empty before."

"Well, there's no one here now," said Summer sadly.

"And I know the reason why," Ellie said grimly. "Look!" She pointed at a snowdrift beside the lake.

Trixi, Summer and Jasmine all turned to look where Ellie was pointing. There, sticking out of the snowdrift, was Queen Malice's horrible black thunderbolt!

Everwarm Embers

"Come on," said Jasmine as they looked at the jagged black shape. "Let's find King Merry and figure out a way to break this nasty thunderbolt."

"We're nearly at the winter palace," Trixi told them reassuringly. Sure enough, as they skied past the lake they could see the royal building ahead.

Even though Ellie was worried about the thunderbolt, she couldn't help admiring the palace. It had one big central tower surrounded by six smaller ones that were connected to it by delicate walkways of sparkling frost. Dozens of snowflake-shaped windows dotted the walls, each with a dusting of snow on the windowsill.

The front door was shaped like a giant snowflake, too. When Trixi knocked on it with her ring, it trembled and made a tinkly sound that echoed around the empty town.

The girls listened as the sound died away, hoping that somebody would come to open the door. But nothing seemed to be moving anywhere in Magic Mountain.

"Where *is* everyone?" fretted Trixi. She flew back from the snowflake door and pointed her ring at it, chanting:

"These girls are here to save the day,
So don't you try to block their way!"

With a creak the door swung open, revealing a grand hallway. But the corridor inside was completely dark!

The three girls took off their skis and
nervously followed Trixi as she flew
ahead into the hall. There were corridors
leading in all directions, and a huge icy
chandelier hung from the ceiling. But
everything was dim and dark. Worse still,
it was almost as cold in here as it had
been outside!

"Hello?" called Ellie. Her voice echoed spookily around the icy walls.

"King Merry?" Jasmine shouted.

Then they heard a noise from a passage on the left.

"That's where the throne room is!" said Trixi in alarm.

The girls hurried off in the direction of the sound.

Summer ran ahead, then stopped and gasped. In front of her was a huge room full of brownies, all huddling together for warmth. Their teeth were chattering and their little faces had turned blue from the cold. In the middle of them all was poor King Merry, shivering hard.

The king looked even rounder than usual. His curly white hair was covered by an enormous furry hat with long ear warmers, and his crown was perched on top of it.

As the girls got closer, they could see why he seemed so tubby – it looked like he was wearing all of his clothes at the same time!

"T-t-Trixi! G-girls! I am so h-happy to s-s-see you," the king stuttered, hugging himself and jiggling on the spot.

"You look freezing!" Summer said sympathetically, rubbing King Merry's arm to warm him up.

"I can help," Trixi said, flying high over the shivering brownies. She started casting spells as quickly as she could. Every time she tapped her ring, a hat or a rolled-up blanket or a pair of cosy woollen socks appeared.

The brownies raised their eyes and watched as colourful woolly hats began drifting down from above. There was one for each of them, printed with the brownie's name and a different snowflake pattern.

As they put the warm hats on and snuggled up in the blankets, the brownies started to look happier and their ears turned bright pink.

"Thank you!" said one brownie, poking his head out from underneath a blanket that had completely covered him. Like his friends, he was about half the girls' height and had bright pink skin, pointy ears and short hair. His hat had *Blizzard* written on it. "Have you come to help us? We've been huddling here all night to keep warm. I was afraid I'd turn into ice!"

"Don't worry," said Jasmine, leaning down to talk to him. "We're here to help. Do you know what's happened?"

"It's the everwarm embers," he said, looking up at her worriedly. "They've all gone out!"

He pointed towards a big fireplace on the other side of the room. It was heaped high with dusty-looking grey lumps. As the girls watched, one of the lumps fell off the top of the pile and tumbled down to the floor. It landed with a sad little thud, and broke into two pieces.

"Even the embers in our necklaces are cold," Blizzard said, holding up a long string that was tied around his neck. At the end of it was a dusty, dim grey stone.

"And if we get too cold, we'll turn to ice!" another brownie said.

The snow brownies looked up at the girls sadly.

"Maybe you could make a fire to heat the embers up?" Ellie suggested to Trixi.

"I'll try," said the little pixie, frowning determinedly. "Stand back!"

She flew up to the fireplace and aimed her ring at it. A stream of crackling red sparks flew out of it and hit the pile of embers, but they stayed grey and dark.

"That settles it," said Trixi, folding her arms and looking cross. "If my magic can't fix it, then it must be the work of that nasty thunderbolt."

"Thunderbolt?" King Merry asked. "Did you find another one?"

"Yes," Jasmine said sadly. "Outside, near Ice-Skate Lake."

"It sounds like my sister is up to no

good again," he frowned. "We have to find a way to break her spell!"

"The other thunderbolts have always shattered when we've stopped Queen Malice from ruining things," Summer said. "Maybe if we can find a way to relight the everwarm embers, that will break Queen Malice's spell!"

"It's daytime now and it's getting warmer," said Ellie. "Couldn't we just pile the embers up in the sunshine?"

"I'm afraid it wouldn't get hot enough to light them, even when it's sunny," said another brownie, whose hat had *Flurry* sewn on it.

All of a sudden, there was a horrible, cackling laugh outside. The girls rushed over to peer out through one of the snowflake-shaped windows. On the other side of the square they saw a huge sleigh, pulled by two wolves with shining red eyes and very big teeth.

A tall, shadowy figure was standing in the sleigh, staring at the palace. She had a pointy crown on her head, which was

perched on top of a mess of frizzy hair.
Her black dress billowed around her in
the cold wind as she raised her spiky staff
to urge the wolves on.

"It's Queen Malice!" whispered Ellie.
"And she's heading this way!" She felt
Blizzard's hand creep into hers, and she
held it tight.

Queen Malice peered in through the snowflake-shaped windows as the sleigh slid by.

"Quick, duck!" Jasmine whispered, bending down so that the queen couldn't see her when she passed by.

Everyone dropped to the floor, their hearts beating fast.

"King Merry!" Trixi whispered, pointing at his head. "Your crown is still too high up. Queen Malice will be able to see it through the window!"

King Merry snatched his crown off, but it was too late.

Suddenly there was a screech of laughter from outside. "It's no use trying to hide, dear brother," Queen Malice called. "I can see your silly little crown!

"There's nothing you or those annoying

human girls can do," she continued. "The everwarm embers have all gone out, and soon your precious little snow brownies will turn into ice lollies. Then there will be no one to look after Magic Mountain, and no one in the Secret Kingdom will be able to have any fun in the snow!"

She laughed again, and the wolves joined in, giving long, moaning howls that made everyone shudder.

"We're not scared of you!" Jasmine shouted, standing up.

"We'll find a way to keep the brownies warm enough!" Ellie added, popping up next to her.

"Oh, no, you won't!" Queen Malice sneered through the window. "Not when it gets even colder!" She turned and pointed her spiky staff at the peak of the mountain, and shot a bolt of lightning into the sky.

The lightning struck a fat grey cloud, pushing it in front of the sun. The sunlight instantly disappeared and the sky turned dim and grey.

Blizzard shivered. "Without the embers and the warm sunshine, we'll turn to ice for sure!" he sobbed.

Summer gave him a hug and then stood up to glare at Queen Malice.

The wicked queen turned and flashed Jasmine, Ellie and Summer a cruel smile, then stamped her staff on the bottom of the sled.

The wolves leapt forward and Queen Malice cackled as she was carried away through the empty streets of Magic Mountain.

"If we don't find a way to relight the everwarm embers soon," Jasmine said with a shiver, "Magic Mountain will be ruined forever!"

Summer's Idea

"We have to save the brownies!" Trixi said, shivering so hard her leaf shook

"But how?" asked Ellie, pulling her green and purple coat tightly around her. "It's so cold I can hardly think!"

"Oh, dear," said Trixi. "There must be something I can do to warm you girls up… I know!"

She tapped her ring and mugs of hot chocolate appeared on the floor in front of everyone. They picked up the mugs gratefully, but as soon as Jasmine took a sip she almost dropped hers to the floor.

"Oh, no!" she said. "It's not hot chocolate, it's *cold* chocolate!"

"Sorry, girls," said Trixi sadly. "I'm so chilly that it's messing up my magic. I can't seem to make anything warm!"

"If only we had the crystal that the people on Cloud Island gave us," said Ellie thoughtfully. "Then we could control the weather and get rid of that snow cloud." She took a step forward – and tripped over something.

"Oops, clumsy clogs!" laughed Jasmine, catching her friend.

"I'm sure this wasn't here a moment ago," said Ellie, bending over to look at the thing she had tripped over. "Hey, it's the Magic Box!" She picked it up and showed it to the others.

"It must have known we needed the crystal!" exclaimed Summer. "Look, it's opening!"

Ellie waited while the lid slowly
rose. Then she lifted out the weather
crystal and held it out in front of her.
The magical jewel glowed as Ellie
held it tightly and thought
about rays of
warm sunshine.
Suddenly
the throne
room grew
lighter and
warmer
as a hole
formed in
the storm
cloud,
letting the
sun shine
through.

"That's better!" Jasmine said as Ellie gently placed the weather crystal back into its space in the Magic Box. With a flash of light and a twinkle the box disappeared.

"Remember, the weather imps told us the crystal's magic won't last for long," Trixi reminded the girls. "We still need to find a way to relight the embers for good!"

Ellie nudged Jasmine and pointed at Summer, who had wandered over to sit beside the cold embers. Her chin was resting on her hand and she looked thoughtful.

"I think Summer's getting an idea," said Ellie.

The two girls walked over and sat down beside their friend. Blizzard and

Flurry came over to sit with them as well.

"There was something my step-dad showed me when we went camping last summer," Summer said. "He showed us a special way to light a fire. It was something to do with sunshine – I wish I could remember what!"

Suddenly Blizzard and Flurry's faces lit up with big smiles.

"We can help with that," grinned Blizzard. "Just watch!"

The two little brownies stood on either side of Summer, who was still gazing at the grey embers. They linked their hands over her head and chanted:

"Brainstorm spell, brainstorm spell,
Summer's thinking very well!"

As they spoke, pink
snowflakes seemed
to appear out
of the air and
dance around
Summer's
head.
Summer's
eyes lit up,
and she
jumped to
her feet. "I
remember now!"
she said. "You can start
a campfire with a magnifying glass. You
hold it in the sunshine and it focuses the
sun's power on one spot so that it gets
really hot – hot enough to start a fire...
or relight some embers!"

Jasmine looked doubtfully at the pile of cold, grey everwarm embers in the fireplace. "But wouldn't we need an incredibly huge magnifying glass?" she asked.

"You can use anything that's really clear," Summer replied, "like a lens from someone's glasses—"

"Or some ice!" Ellie chimed in, catching on to Summer's idea.

"We could use the ice from Ice-Skate Lake!" cried Jasmine.

"Yes, that's perfect!" said Summer.

"That might just work!" said Blizzard, grinning at the girls.

The other brownies cheered.

"Let's get moving," said Jasmine. "We don't know how long the weather crystal's sunshine spell will last, and we have lots to do before the sun disappears behind that nasty storm cloud again."

The girls explained their plan to Trixi and the king, and they all rushed out of the palace and headed towards the lake.

"Won't the ice just melt in the sun?" King Merry asked, looking up at the bright rays glowing down from behind the hole in the storm cloud.

"I don't think so," said Summer. "My step-dad's magnifying glass didn't get hot – it just pushed all the heat onto the campfire."

"Oh, splendid!" said the king, clutching his robes around himself more tightly as they walked out into the windy street. "Ingenious! So we put the everwarm embers in the lake to ice up!"

"Um, no," said Ellie. "I think what

Summer said was—"

The king shook his hands in the air, as if to say that he finally understood.

"Ah, I see, I see!" he said. "We ice the sun to melt the embers!"

"Er, not quite," Jasmine told him.

The king looked bewildered.

"Why don't we stop and rest for a while, Your Majesty?" said Trixi. "I'll explain it to you."

She raised her tiny eyebrows at the girls. "You go on ahead," she whispered to them. "This could take a while!"

The three friends giggled and ran ahead with the brownies to put their plan into action. But as they hurried on, they heard poor King Merry getting more and more confused behind them.

"We're going to melt the sun with ice-skates…no, put the sun in the everwarm embers…no… Oh, dear. I'll never sort this out!"

A Race Against Time

By the time the girls and the brownies got to the town square, they had a plan in place.

First, Summer stood in front of everyone and explained her idea to make a giant lens out of ice. Then Jasmine sent teams of brownies off to visit every

café and igloo in Magic Mountain to
gather up all the everwarm embers from
the fireplaces and necklaces and bring
them back to the town square. Finally,
Trixi and the girls led another group of
brownies to Ice-Skate Lake to work on
making the ice lens.

"How are we going to cut such a big
chunk out of the ice?" Ellie asked as they
walked toward the lake. "Can you do it
with your magic, Trixi?"

"That's a job for the brownies!" replied
the pixie. "They can sculpt and shape ice,
remember? Just wait and see."

When the group reached Ice-Skate
Lake, all the nearby brownies except for
Blizzard arranged themselves in a circle
around the frozen bank.

Blizzard strapped on a pair of skates

and skimmed out across the ice, looking
very serious. He skated around in a circle,
leaving a deep cut in the surface.

The brownies at the edge of the lake
began a quiet chant that sounded like
gently falling snow. Then there was a
loud crack, and the disc of ice broke
away from the lake and rose up into
the air. It spun over and over in the

air, slowly changing shape until it was curved on both sides like the lens of a magnifying glass.

Trixi pointed her ring at the ice lens, and it began to float slowly in the direction of the town square.

"I wish I could make things out of ice like that!" Ellie told Blizzard admiringly as they all set off towards town.

"It's special snow brownie magic," said Blizzard proudly. "You're the first humans ever to see us do it!"

When they got back to the town square, the girls helped the rest of the brownies pile the final embers onto a heap in the middle of a big patch of sunlight streaming through the hole in the cloud.

"Does the hole look smaller to you?"

Jasmine asked as she squinted up at it.

"Yes," Summer replied with a worried frown. "The weather crystal's magic must be wearing off."

"The ice lens is here!" Ellie called as she ran up to them.

Trixi pointed her ring at the floating ice lens and moved it through the air until it hovered between the sun and the pile of embers.

Summer waved her arms to help direct Trixi. They had to get the lens in exactly the right position, or the plan wouldn't work. They turned it left and right and tilted it backwards and forwards, but they just couldn't seem to get the sunshine to focus on the embers.

All the brownies huddled together anxiously as they looked up at hole

in the snow cloud, which was getting
smaller every minute. Any moment now,
the weather crystal's magic would wear
off and the snow cloud would cover the
sun again!

"Come on, come on!" chanted Flurry,
jumping up and down anxiously, willing
the lens to catch the sun.

"This is too much for me!" moaned
King Merry. He sat down in the snow
and covered his eyes. His crown fell off
and landed upside down in the pink snow
beside him.

Suddenly Ellie saw a flash of light
as the lens focused the sun's rays for a
moment. "Back there!" she shouted to
Trixi and Summer. "Left a bit!"

As Trixi tilted the slab of ice to the
left, the sunlight finally beamed through

its centre. Sunshine streamed onto the
embers, bathing them in heat.

"Look, King Merry!" Jasmine gasped.
"It's working!"

Just as she finished speaking, there
was a soft little *pop*. A bright red glow
appeared at the very top of the big pile.
The first ember was alight!

Another followed, then another and another. Now all the embers at the top of the pile were shining warmly. The little cracking sounds continued as more and more embers came back to life. The brownies squealed with excitement and danced around the heap of embers, stretching their little pink fingers out to feel the heat.

Trixi flew happily around the edge of the pile a few times, holding her hands out in the warm air.

Once she had warmed up, she came back
to hover beside King Merry and the girls.
Then she tapped her ring and conjured
everyone up their own enormous two-
handled mug full of steaming hot
chocolate. Each mug had a sparkly
magic marshmallow the size of a fairy
cake in it!

"Mmm, just what I wanted!" sighed
Ellie. She took a big slurp from her cup
and licked off the chocolate moustache it
left behind on her lip.

"Ahhh," sighed the king happily,
gulping his hot chocolate.

By now the entire pile of embers was
shining red and yellow with heat.

"Look!" said Summer, pointing up
at the afternoon sky. "The reindeer are
coming back!"

The magnificent flying herd swooped in low over the pile of embers, warming their bellies. Their glossy coats shone in the red and yellow light.

"Watch out!" one called as he swooped by. "On the mountain!"

"What do you mean?" called Jasmine, but the reindeer had already flown away.

The girls heard one last *pop* from the heat — the final ember catching light — followed by an enormous *crack!* that echoed around the valley.

"What was that?" Ellie asked her friends, covering her ears as the sound bounced off the igloos and the walls of the winter palace.

"I think it was Queen Malice's thunderbolt breaking!" said Jasmine, racing towards the lake to look.

Ellie, Summer, Trixi and the brownies followed behind. When they got to the spot where the thunderbolt had been, all they could see were little black shards scattered on the pink snow.

"We've broken the spell!" Jasmine cried.

A huge shout rose from the crowd of brownies. They all hugged one another, then came forward to take their necklaces from the pile.

Blizzard gave necklaces to
Jasmine, Summer and
Ellie, and the girls
put them on,
smiling as they
felt the heat
of the ember
warming them
right through.

"Hooray!"
smiled Blizzard.
"Thank you, Summer,
Ellie and Jasmine!" All the brownies
started cheering again.

Suddenly the cheering was drowned out
by a horrible chorus of cackling laughter.
The noise seemed to be coming from

higher up the mountain.

As everyone looked up, they saw that a huge group of Storm Sprites was snowboarding down towards them, holding buckets full of water.

"The thunderbolt may be broken, but we're not giving up!" one sprite called down.

"Yeah!" said another. "We're going to soak those everwarm embers and put them out for good!"

The sprites howled with laughter as they raced toward the town square, holding their buckets ready.

"Oh, no!" Flurry gasped. "If the embers get wet before they're up to full strength, we might never be able to light them again!"

Snowboarding Sprites

"Don't worry!" Blizzard grinned. "I know how to handle this." He scooped up an armful of snow, and before the girls had time to say anything, there was a neat pile of snowballs on the ground. Blizzard picked one up and threw it at the nearest sprite, hitting him right on the nose!

"Good idea!" Summer giggled, throwing one of the snowy lumps at a sprite as he whizzed by.

Everyone started to pick up snowballs and hurl them at the sprites. Even Trixi joined in the fight, using her pixie magic to send snowballs flying towards the nasty creatures, and knocking three of them over with one blast from her ring!

Flurry gave a low whistle, and seconds later the herd of flying reindeer landed in the square. He and some other brownies rushed towards the reindeer and jumped on their backs.

"Come on!" Flurry called to the girls.

"I think I'll stay here on solid ground!" Ellie replied, shaking her head and throwing a snowball at the same time.

Summer and Jasmine threw one more snowball each and then ran over to the waiting animals.

"Go ahead and climb up," one of the reindeer told Summer with a smile.

"Thank you!" Summer breathed, gently stroking his velvety nose. She quickly clambered up onto his strong back and wrapped her arms around his neck.

"This is going to be great!" Jasmine said as she climbed up on another reindeer.

Blizzard made another pile of snowballs and gave everyone an armful before hopping on a reindeer. "Let's go!" he called.

The reindeer raced off along the road, and then suddenly lifted right off the snow and into the air!

"We're flying!" Summer squealed. She held on tight as her reindeer flew over the snowboarding sprites.

"Take that!" Jasmine shouted gleefully as she pelted a Storm Sprite from above.

"And that!" Summer joined in, flying nearby.

The sprite squealed as the snowballs rained down from above.

Ellie saw her chance, and launched a surprise attack from in front of him, throwing a snowball that hit him right in his middle. "And THAT!" she yelled triumphantly.

The sprite fell over and dropped his bucket, splashing water everywhere. "Hey!" he wailed, half-covered in snow.

"Get out of my way, Big-Ears!" shouted another sprite snowboarding behind him.

"You get out of *my* way, Stinky-Shorts!" snapped the first sprite.

But the snowboarding sprite was going too fast to stop, and he fell straight over the one on the ground! His bucket of water flew high in the air and landed on the big-eared sprite's head.

As the girls watched, the two sprites started rolling down the hill in a tangle of skinny grey arms and legs, collecting more and more snow as they went.

"Aaah!" another sprite squealed as the giant snowball picked up speed behind him.

He desperately tried to snowboard out of the way, but he got caught up too!

The snowball continued to tumble down the mountain, rolling over sprites as it went. It gradually began to slow down as it crossed the town square, and then it landed in a big heap a few metres from the pile of everwarm embers.

Ellie, Trixi, King Merry and the brownies cheered. Summer and Jasmine's reindeer flew in circles to celebrate, then landed gently. Summer, Jasmine and Blizzard ran over to the others, their faces flushed with excitement.

"That was amazing!" Summer grinned. "And we stopped those nasty sprites!"

The girls all looked at the sprites. They were still lying in a pile of snow, looking very dizzy.

"We'll make sure they can't bother us any more," Blizzard said with a grin.

He and the other snow brownies went over and formed a circle around the sprites, then started their low chanting again. Suddenly the sprites went very still, and pink icicles formed on their noses and their bony fingers.

"We're turning them into ice statues for a little while," Blizzard told the girls. "It won't hurt them, but it should keep them out of mischief!"

Just then they heard a shriek from high up on the mountain slope. The girls looked up and could just make out a dark shape at the mountain's peak. It was Queen Malice's wolf-sled. The queen was standing up in the back, shaking her fist in fury.

"You girls haven't seen the last of me, or my thunderbolts!" she screeched. "I'll ruin all the fun in the Secret Kingdom – just you wait and see!" And with that, she stamped her thunderbolt staff and the wolf-sled sped away.

At that moment it suddenly got dark, and fat pink flakes started falling from the sky.

"The snow cloud!" exclaimed Ellie, pointing up at the sky.

The others looked up just in time to see the gap in the cloud close. The weather crystal's spell had broken, and now Queen Malice's horrible snow cloud completely covered the sun.

"Quick," said Summer. "We have to get embers back into all the buildings to keep them warm!"

Summer, Ellie and Jasmine rushed around the town, helping the brownies put an everwarm ember in every home, and in all the lanterns around Ice-Skate Lake. The pink ice glimmered beautifully in the glowing light, and Ellie, Jasmine and Summer stood and watched the snow falling onto it.

"It doesn't matter how cold it gets now!" Summer said cheerfully. "The everwarm embers will keep everyone nice and cosy!"

Flurry rushed over, beaming happily. "All the embers are in place," he declared. "Would you like to come to a snowball café and have something to eat?"

Ellie, Summer and Jasmine looked at one another and grinned. "Yes, please!" they all said at the same time.

Soon the girls were snuggled cosily in a snowball café, sitting around a fireplace full of everwarm embers and eating special, warm ice cream puddings that had been magically baked on the embers.

"Look!" Ellie said, pointing outside.

The Storm Sprites had thawed out and were jumping up and down and rubbing their arms, trying to get warm. As the girls watched, one of them stuck out his tongue and blew a raspberry at them.

Trixi sighed. "They don't seem to have learnt their lesson. They're just as rude and naughty as ever!"

Everyone crowded around the window and watched as the sprites flapped away.

"It's stopped snowing!" Blizzard realised, pointing outside. "Let's go and have some winter fun!"

All the brownies leapt up and ran outside.

"Come on, girls!" Flurry called as he headed out the door. "Now we can show you just how magical Magic Mountain really is!"

Snowy Fun!

Summer stared around in amazement. The snow had only just stopped, but suddenly there were brownies sledding, skiing and snowboarding everywhere she looked! "Everyone's having such a good time!" she giggled.

"That's all thanks to you," said Flurry. "And now you get to enjoy Magic Mountain too!"

"Didn't you say you wanted to go on
the ice slides?" Trixi asked Jasmine.

"Oh, yes please!" Jasmine shrieked.

"Then follow us," called Blizzard as he
and Flurry led the girls to a wire with
lots of funny benches dangling from it.
"These will take us up to the ice slides!"
he said, pointing to the benches, which
were moving slowly up the mountain. He
and Jasmine jumped onto the first chair
and were scooped away.

"Wheeee!" Jasmine cried as the chair
went up the mountain.

Flurry and Ellie sat on the next chair
and Summer followed with King Merry.
Soon they were all being carried up
the mountain towards the ice slides,
which twisted down the slopes like giant
helter-skelters.

"Oh, dear," muttered Ellie, when she saw how high up they were.

"Don't be scared," Flurry said as they reached the top and jumped off the chairlift. "You just sit on the slide and whoosh all the way down – it's fun!"

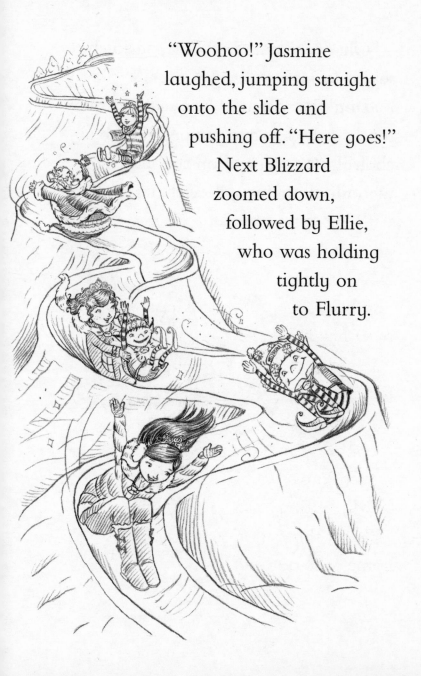

"Woohoo!" Jasmine
laughed, jumping straight
onto the slide and
pushing off. "Here goes!"
Next Blizzard
zoomed down,
followed by Ellie,
who was holding
tightly on
to Flurry.

King Merry slipped as he sat down and ended up going down the whole slide bottom-first! Summer came close behind him, giggling as she went.

After the slide, Jasmine lay down in the pink snow and made an angel shape with her arms and legs. "I'd like to play in the snow every day!" she said happily.

"Ooh, I don't think I would," said Ellie. "It's been lovely to visit Magic Mountain, but I like being warm!"

"I like everywhere in the Secret Kingdom," said Summer. She gave a big yawn. "But right now I'm looking forward to snuggling up in bed."

Trixi looked at the sun, which was slowly getting lower in the sky.

"Yes, I think it's time for you to go home," she agreed.

"I suppose so," said Jasmine reluctantly. "Can we come back soon?"

"I certainly hope you will," King Merry replied, nodding so hard that his crown slipped down over one eye. "I don't know how I'd handle my frightful sister without you!"

The king got up and hugged each girl in turn, and

Trixi gave them all a tiny kiss on the nose.

"Ahem!" coughed Blizzard loudly. Everyone turned to look at the little brownie, who blushed bright red.

Then Flurry gave him a poke, and he held up his arms to Summer. He had an icy pink hourglass in his little hand. "Um…"

mumbled Blizzard. He seemed to get a little braver as he saw everyone smiling at him. "King Merry agreed we should give this to you as a thank-you present. It's an icy hourglass. It freezes time for a little while."

"Like this," said Flurry, taking the hourglass from his friend and turning it over. Immediately everything froze still. Flurry took Blizzard's hat off and put it on back to front. When Flurry flipped the hourglass again, everything un-froze.

"Hey!" Blizzard grumbled, realising that his hat was on backwards.

The girls giggled.

"Thank you," said Jasmine, taking the hourglass. "I'm sure this will be useful during our adventures!"

Ellie, Summer and Jasmine said goodbye

to everyone, and then Trixi tapped her
ring. A magic whirlwind began to form
around them, sweeping them away as the
brownies waved goodbye.

When they opened their eyes again,
everything was dark. Their outdoor
clothes were gone, and they could feel
sleeping bags underneath their bare feet.

Summer lifted the Magic Box down
from her shelf and put it on her bed.
With a flurry of sparkling lights, the box
opened, revealing the six compartments
inside. Jasmine carefully slipped the
hourglass in next to the weather crystal.
It fitted perfectly!

Summer got up again to place the box back on its shelf. "What a lovely adventure we had," she sighed, crawling under her duvet. Suddenly she felt very tired. "And now there's only one thunderbolt left to find. Where do you think we'll go next?"

But there was no reply from her two friends – they were already fast asleep.

In the next Secret Kingdom adventure, Ellie, Summer and Jasmine visit

Glitter Beach

Read on for a sneak peek...

The Adventure Begins

"Hi, Mum! I'm home!"

Ellie Macdonald ran into the empty kitchen through the back door. She shrugged her schoolbag off her shoulders and put it down carefully. After all, there was something very special inside! At the bottom, wrapped up in her school jumper, was a mysterious wooden box.

As she opened her bag, Ellie felt a flicker of excitement. She and her best friends, Summer and Jasmine, were the only ones who knew that the box was much more than an ordinary jewellery box. It had been made by the ruler of a magical land called the Secret Kingdom, where incredible creatures like fairies, mermaids, unicorns and pixies lived. It was a wonderful place, but it was in terrible trouble.

When everyone in the land had decided they wanted kind King Merry to rule rather than his horrid sister, Queen Malice, the evil queen had sent six thunderbolts crashing into different parts of the kingdom. Each thunderbolt had the power to make trouble and bring great unhappiness. Ellie and her friends had promised to help stop the nasty queen. Whenever one of her thunderbolts caused a problem in the Secret Kingdom, a riddle would appear in the lid of the Magic Box to tell the girls where they were needed. When they had solved it, Ellie, Summer and Jasmine would be whisked away to the kingdom to try and help. They had already had five wonderful adventures and Ellie couldn't wait for the magic to work again!

Ellie pulled the Magic Box out of her bag and looked hopefully at the carvings of amazing creatures that covered every side, and the glittering jewels that decorated its mirrored lid. If only the lid would start glowing, that would mean it was time for her and her friends to return to the Secret Kingdom. But all she could see was her own reflection, her red curls falling messily around her face.

Ellie sighed and carried the box to the hall carefully. She caught sight of her mum through the window, tidying up the hanging baskets in the front garden. Ellie avoided her and headed for the stairs, clutching the Magic Box.

"RARRRRR!" With a loud yell, Molly, Ellie's little sister, jumped out from where she had been hiding beside the hall table.

Ellie almost dropped the box in shock. "Molly!"

Molly whooped in delight. "I made you jump, Ellie!" She was four and looked just like Ellie had when she was little, with red curls that reached to her shoulders and mischievous green eyes. She loved to play tricks on her big sister. "What's that?" she said curiously, spotting the box in Ellie's arms.

"Nothing."

"Let me see!" Molly tried to look.

"It's just an old box, Mol," Ellie told her hastily. The last thing she wanted was Molly looking in the Magic Box! Inside it were six wooden compartments, and five of them were filled with the special objects Ellie and the others had collected on their adventures.

There was a magic map of the Secret Kingdom, a tiny silver unicorn horn that let the person holding it talk to animals, a cloud crystal that could be used to control the weather, a pearl that could turn you invisible and an icy hourglass that could be used to freeze time.

If Molly found those things she'd want to know where they had come from and the girls couldn't tell anyone about the Secret Kingdom!

Read
Glitter Beach
to find out what
happens next!

Be in on the secret. Collect them all!

Enjoy six sparkling adventures.

Out now!

Secret Kingdom

A magical world of friendship and fun!

Join best friends
Ellie, Summer and Jasmine at

www.secretkingdombooks.com

and enjoy games, sneak peeks
and lots more!

You'll find great activities, competitions, stories
and games, plus a special newsletter for
Secret Kingdom friends!

Character Profile:

Trixibelle

(also known as Trixi)

Personality:
Bubbly and practical.
Trixi is always there to
help King Merry —
and Summer, Jasmine
and Ellie too!

**Favourite
place in the
Secret Kingdom:**
Glitter Beach, where once
a year the sand turns to
glitter dust.

Friendship Quiz

Summer, Ellie and Jasmine have been friends since they were little, and they've made lots more friends in the Secret Kingdom. But if you went to the Secret Kingdom, who would your best friend be? Take our quiz to find out!

Do you like your friends to be...?

A – kind
B – magical
C – mean

What would you like to do with your best friend?

A – sit on a snuggly throne
B – cast spells
C – throw horrible thunderbolts at people

If your best friend was scared of something, what would it be?

A – stink toads
B – not being able to protect her friends
C – nothing, because everyone is scared of her

Which place would you like to visit with your friend?

A – a beautiful enchanted palace
B – a glittering beach
C – a dark and scary castle

If your best friend had a favourite hobby, what would it be?

A – inventing magical devices
B – helping friends in need
C – making other people sad

Mostly As

Your best friend is King Merry!
King Merry needs a lot of
looking after, but he's a very
kind best friend. And he has
a whole kingdom
to play in!

Mostly Bs

Your best friend is Trixi!
Trixi is a helpful best friend who
can use her pixie magic to get
anything you need!

Mostly Cs

Your best friend is Queen Malice!
You can have lots of fun with
Queen Malice, as long as you enjoy
making other people miserable!

Secret Kingdom Codebreaker

Sssh! Can you keep a secret? Ellie, Summer and Jasmine have written a special message just for you!
They have written one secret word of their special message in each of the six Secret Kingdom books.

To discover the secret word, hold a small mirror to this page and see your word
magically appear!

The first secret word is: _____

When you have cracked the code and found all six secret words,
work out the special message and go online to enter the competition at

www.secretkingdombooks.com

We will put all of the correct entries into a draw and select one winner to receive a special
Secret Kingdom goody bag featuring lots of sparkly gifts, including a glittery t-shirt!

You can also send your entry on a postcard to:

Secret Kingdom Competition, Orchard Books, 338 Euston Road, London, NW1 3BH

Don't forget to include your name and address.

Good luck!

Closing Date: 31st October 2012.

Collect the tokens from each Secret Kingdom book to get special Secret Kingdom gifts!

In every Secret Kingdom book there are three Friendship Tokens that you can exchange for special gifts! Send your friendship tokens in to us as soon as you get them or save them up to get an even more special gift!

3 tokens   **5** tokens   **7** tokens   **13** tokens   **15** tokens

Secret Kingdom poster and collectable glittery bookmark

Pencil and rubber set

Pocket mirror

Two best friends friendship bracelets (one for you and one for your best friend)

Glittery t-shirt

To take part in this offer, please send us a letter telling us why you like Secret Kingdom. Don't forget to:
1) Tell us which gift you would like to exchange your tokens for
2) Include the correct number of Friendship Tokens for each gift you are requesting
3) Include your name and address
4) Include the signature of a parent or guardian

Secret Kingdom Friendship Token Offer
Orchard Books Marketing Department
338 Euston Road, London, NW1 3BH

Closing date: 31st October 2012

www.secretkingdombooks.com

1 Friendship Token	1 Friendship Token	1 Friendship Token
www.secretkingdombooks.com	www.secretkingdombooks.com	www.secretkingdombooks.com